For Pippo.
– ZH

For Mollie and Lara.
– DGB

The Pocket Chaotic

Text © Ziggy Hanaor
Illustrations © Daniel Gray-Barnett

British Library Cataloguing-in-Publication Data.

A CIP record for this book is
available from the British Library.
ISBN: 978-1-908714-80-0

First published in the UK, 2020
and USA, 2021, by Cicada Books Ltd.

Printed in the United Kingdom.

Cicada Books Ltd
48 Burghley Road
London, NW5 1UE
www.cicadabooks.co.uk

The Pocket
CHAOTIC

WRITTEN BY
ZIGGY HANAOR

ILLUSTRATED BY
DANIEL GRAY-BARNETT

Alexander's mum, Nancy,
was good at lots of things:

She was great at skipping rope,

a fine cook,

a talented pianist.

and a fabulous crafter.

Alexander loved
hanging out with her.
She was, without a
doubt, the best mum
in the world.

But she was *not* the neatest
mum in the world.

She was always knocking things over,
and mixing things up, and losing things.

For the most part, Alexander didn't mind,
but there was one thing that really drove him crazy...

She was always putting stuff
in her pouch. And her pouch
was where Alexander spent
most of his time.

She would keep her phone and
her wallet in there. Fair enough. But that
was just the beginning.

When they went to the shops, she'd drop
her change and her receipts into her pouch,
without putting them away.

When they went to the park, she'd pick up
a nice feather and a smooth stone in the shape
of a heart, and stick them in her pouch.

When they picked up Alexander's sister, Elly, from school, she'd shove the school newsletter, a cereal bar wrapper and Elly's old gym shorts into her pouch.

'Ugh,' said Alexander, 'this stinks!'
'Stop being such a baby,' said Elly. 'I left mum's pocket when I was way younger than you.'

But Alexander liked it in the pocket.
It was cosy and warm, and it smelled so
reassuringly of Mum.

Alexander did his best to keep things tidy,
but it was hard to stay on top of it all.

Alexander sighed. 'Why can't you be more like Isabella's mum? She is always neat as a pin.'

'Sorry, love,' said Nancy, as she dropped in a handful of sweets and a comb.

So Alexander got more organised.

He started a filing system and put everything away in alphabetical order.

But the more he filed,
the more stuff poured in.

'Maybe if you carried a briefcase, like Daniel's dad, it would be easier to keep things tidy,' said Alexander.

'Daniel's dad doesn't even *have* a pouch,' sneered Elly, as she hopped away.

Then one Wednesday, it got really bad:

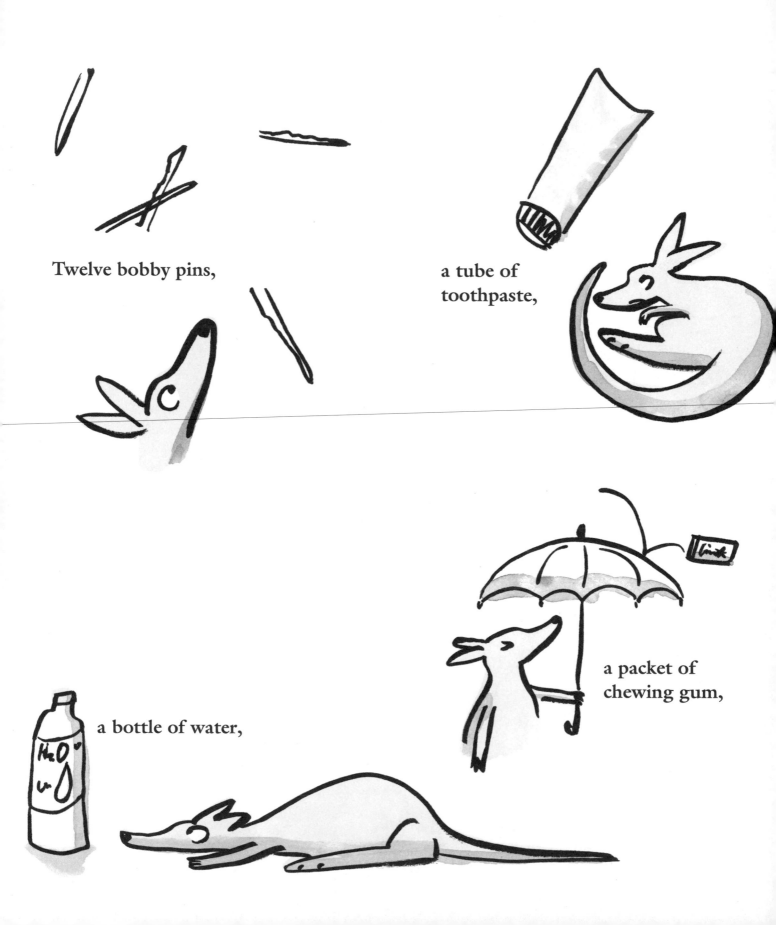

Twelve bobby pins,

a tube of
toothpaste,

a packet of
chewing gum,

a bottle of water,

two bus tickets,

some keys,

a toy car

and a
cookbook

all found their way into Nancy's pouch.

Alexander barely had room to move, but his mum couldn't seem to stop. In came:

A pair of socks

a jar of honey

A recorder

a box of tissues

three pencils

a skipping rope

A HALF.

EATEN.

BANANA.

'I'VE HAD ENOUGH!' shouted Alexander.
'This pocket is too CHAOTIC!'

'Too what?' asked Nancy.

'Too chaotic! It's a mess and
there's no room for me any more.
I'm MOVING OUT!'

So Alexander moved into the
bedroom next to Elly's, and actually
it wasn't so bad.

Mum sewed him a furry blanket to make his bed cosy.

They put up shelves, so that Alexander could keep all his things neat and tidy.

And Mum gave him one of her old scarves that smelled Mum-like and reassuring.

So his bed was just like her pocket.

Almost.